KU-780-452

Stewart Lees
RUNAWAY JACK

FRANCES LINCOLN CHILDREN'S BOOKS

"Grandpa, what's this?"

Isaac was staring into his grandfather's cabinet.

"That, Isaac, is Jack's little wooden horse."

"Who's Jack?" asked Isaac.

"Jack was your great-great-great-grandfather.

Sit down, and I'll tell you the story…"

Jack always looked out for his kid sister Molly. As babies, they'd been taken from their ma and pa and sold. This was back in the days of slavery.

Their new master was a tobacco planter in Mayfield, Kentucky. He had the two children raised by a kindly couple called Rachel and Daniel. Rachel worked in the big kitchen and Daniel looked after the master's stables.

The two children enjoyed helping out. They were better off than most, I guess, but all that was about to change...

The sun was rising as a wagon bounced and rattled its way out of the estate.

"Where are they taking us, Daniel?" asked Jack.

Daniel looked up. There were tears in his eyes.

"To the courthouse, Jack," he said. "We're all going to be sold, to settle the master's debts."

That night, Jack pressed something into Molly's hand. "I've made this for you, Molly. If we get split up tomorrow, it will remind you of me."

Molly opened her hand and saw lying there a small wooden horse.

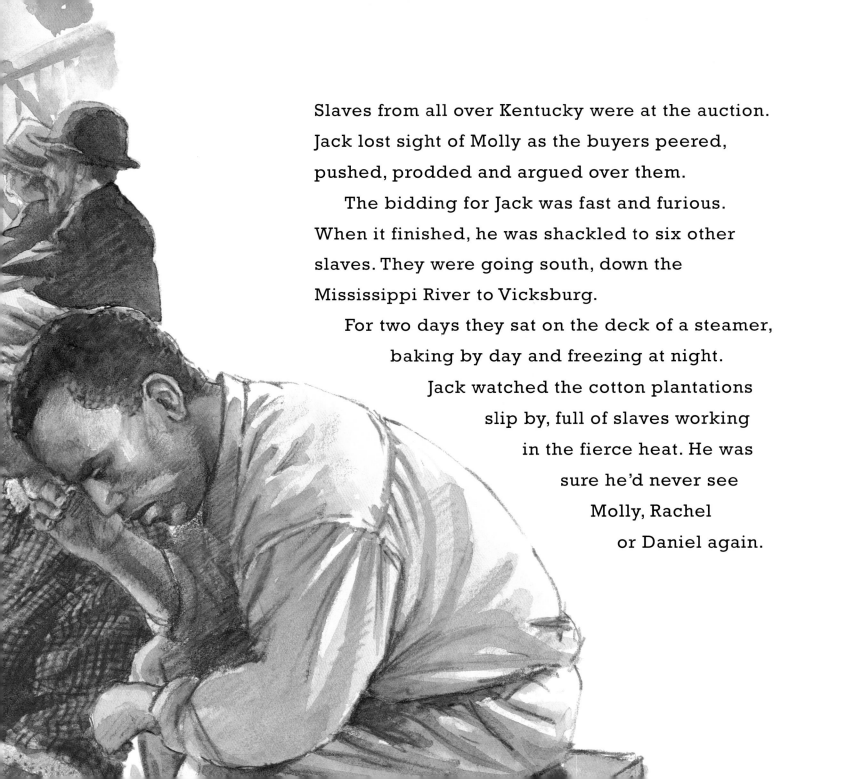

Slaves from all over Kentucky were at the auction. Jack lost sight of Molly as the buyers peered, pushed, prodded and argued over them.

The bidding for Jack was fast and furious. When it finished, he was shackled to six other slaves. They were going south, down the Mississippi River to Vicksburg.

For two days they sat on the deck of a steamer, baking by day and freezing at night.

Jack watched the cotton plantations slip by, full of slaves working in the fierce heat. He was sure he'd never see Molly, Rachel or Daniel again.

Jack was put to work with a party of women picking cotton. At the end of each long day he lay down, aching and tired, and cried himself to sleep.

Anyone who didn't pick their daily quota of cotton was beaten.

"I saw you putting some of your cotton in Sally's bag," Jack whispered to a woman one day.

"Keep it quiet, Jack. If the overseer finds out, we'll all be whipped. Sally's not as young and strong as the rest of us."

After that, Jack always put some of his cotton into Sally's bag.

One hot day, Sally had to rest.

"On your feet!" shouted the overseer, raising his whip.

Jack could bear it no longer. He grabbed the whip from the overseer and threw it as far as he could.

What had he done?

Terrified, he turned and ran, blindly crashing through fields of cotton. The fields turned to wet marshland, but he didn't stop. Behind him, men were giving chase, the barking of their dogs growing louder.

He scrambled up a bank – and suddenly there was nowhere left to run because there, stretching before him in the fading light, lay the vast Mississippi.

Upriver, Jack could see a small town. He picked
his way along the water's edge towards it.
But angry shouts told him that his pursuers had
got there ahead of him.

   His heart thumping, he crouched by the landing
where a ferry sat moored up for the night.

   Looking round, he had an idea. He slipped into
the water and hauled himself up on to the ferry's
crowded cargo deck. Then he climbed in amongst
the cotton bales and pulled another bale across.
Now he was completely hidden.

Soon the silence on board was shattered. Jack held his breath as a voice close by boomed, "Search this area!"

All at once, Jack's hiding-place was flooded with moonlight as a bale was lifted. Jack looked up, startled. Above him, an equally surprised young face looked down. Then, without a word, the bale was replaced.

Jack waited until all was quiet again before daring to poke his head out.

But immediately he froze. SOMEONE WAS BEHIND HIM!

"I guess you're the runaway everyone's so excited about."

It was the young face from earlier. Jack nodded.

"Listen," said the boy. "Near here are some folks called Quakers. They might help you get up north."

So the next day, at one of the ferry stops, Jack slipped over the side and climbed ashore. He waited until sundown, then struck out across country. But as he emerged from the darkness into the light of a homestead, a voice cried, "Who goes there?" and a hand held him firmly by the shoulder.

"Don't struggle, lad. We won't harm thee – we're Quakers," said the man. "We're keeping watch for slave hunters. We've been looking after a runaway family and they're leaving tonight."

Outside the house, a man and a woman with a child were being helped into a carriage. As he passed them, Jack tripped on something, and he bent to pick it up.

"That's mine!" cried the child. But Jack wasn't listening – because, as his hand closed over it, he felt the smooth, familiar shape of his little wooden horse.

Looking up, he let out a cry. It was Molly! And the man and woman standing behind her were Rachel and Daniel!

"So they were the runaway family!" cried Isaac.

"That's right," said his grandfather. "They all missed Jack badly, and Daniel got to thinking that maybe, if they reached the north, they could save some money, find Jack and buy him his freedom."

"What happened then?" asked Isaac.

"Well, the Quakers helped them along the Underground Railroad to Chicago, where they were free, and Daniel and Rachel settled and raised the two children there.

And this story has been handed down along with the little wooden horse that brought them all together again."

About the Story

The Mississippi steamboat carried Jack through some of the most dangerous territory for any runaway slave during the 1840s – the lower southern states of America. This was an area full of slave-hunters and suspicious local people, where a runaway would almost certainly be recaptured.

Slaves were a valuable commodity, for this was a golden age in the deep south and the economy was booming. Since the invention of the cotton-gin the cotton plantations had expanded rapidly, creating a huge demand for labour. And then, in 1811, the first light-draft steamboat succeeded in sailing upstream through the strong Mississippi currents. The southern sugar producers suddenly found the valuable markets in the north opening up to them. The result was that the slave population of the southern states mushroomed from just over 100,000 in 1790 to 2,500,000 by 1850.

In the upper southern states, though, falling tobacco prices meant that the plantations of Virginia and Kentucky struggled to survive. It had been illegal since 1808 to import new slaves from Africa, and so, many slaves like Jack found themselves being sold down the river.

For Rachel, Daniel and the two children, the next 350 miles to Chicago and freedom were still fraught with danger, but now they would receive food and shelter from sympathisers on the famous "Underground Railroad". Many of these sympathisers were Quakers, members of a Christian Protestant sect formed 150 years earlier in England. They campaigned for many social reforms including the abolition of slavery.

Jack was to return to the deep South just fifteen years later, this time as a soldier. He joined the Union army, which was struggling to defeat the armies of the Southern Confederacy – the last stronghold of American slavery. When the Civil War ended in 1865, the victorious Union passed the Thirteenth Amendment that finally ended slavery throughout the United States of America.